DreamWorks & Aardman

Flushed Away™

PLUMBING PROBLEMS

Adapted by Sarah Durkee

Pencils by Mike Morris   Color by Barry Gott

Scholastic Inc.

New York   Toronto   London   Auckland   Sydney
Mexico City   New Delhi   Hong Kong   Buenos Aires

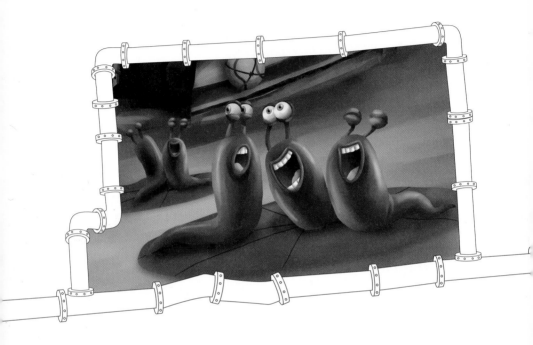

ISBN-13: 978-0-439-90077-5
ISBN-10: 0-439-90077-8

Flushed Away © 2006 DreamWorks Animation L.L.C. and Aardman Animations Ltd.
Flushed Away™ DreamWorks Animation L.L.C.

Published by Scholastic Inc.
SCHOLASTIC and associated logos are trademarks and/or registered trademarks of Scholastic Inc.

12 11 10 9 8 7 6 5 4 3 2 1   7 8 9 10

Designed by Paul W. Banks
Printed in the U.S.A.
First printing, November 2006

Roderick St. James was living the good life. His home was like a palace. He wore the finest clothes. He even drove a fancy car. Roddy had everything that a pet rat could want.

One night, Roddy heard a strange noise.
He went to see what it was. He found a big,
dirty, scruffy rat.

"The name's Sid," growled the rat.
"I'm staying here to watch the World Cup,
GOT IT?"

Roddy had a plan to get rid of Sid, but it didn't work. Instead of flushing Sid down the toilet, Roddy was the one who got flushed.

"Bon voyage!" Sid said as Roddy disappeared.

Roddy flew down the pipes, twisting and turning. Finally he landed in a dark tunnel. He stood up and came face-to-face with a slimy slug. "Aaaaahhhhhh!" he screamed.

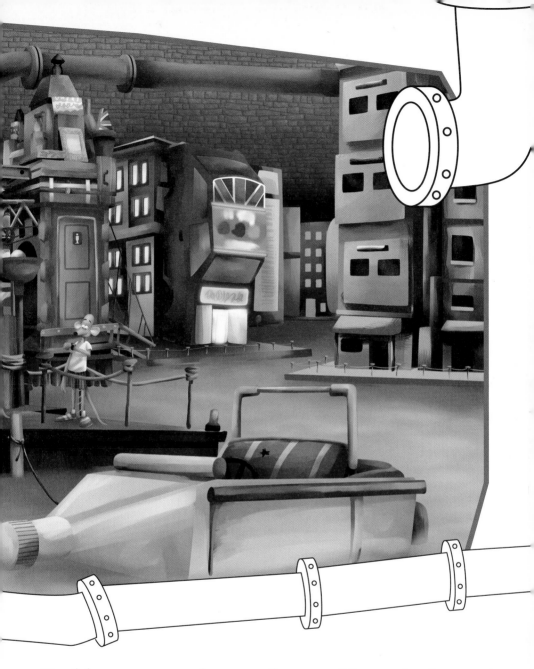

Roddy ran toward a metal grate. He pushed through it and there, on the other side, was . . . an entire underground city!

"What is this place?" he asked. "How am I going to get home?"

Roddy was told to find a ship called the *Jammy Dodger.*

"What are you doing on my boat?" Captain Rita asked.

"Someone said you could help me get home," Roddy explained.

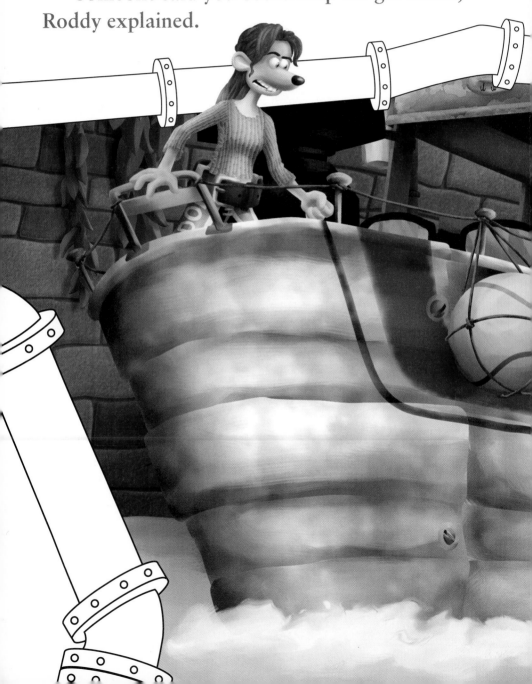

"Listen, I've got my own problems, mate," Rita whispered. She clapped a hand over Roddy's mouth and pulled him into the shadows.

"There's rats out there who'd like to kill me," she said.

Just then, a tough gang of rats climbed aboard the *Jammy Dodger*.

"Rita, Rita, Rita, you thought you could give us the slip, eh?" said Spike, the smallest rat. "Where's The Toad's ruby?"

"I don't have his stupid ruby!" Rita yelled. "He stole it from me," she said, pointing at Roddy.

"I did not!" Roddy shouted. "Look at her bottom!"

Whitey the rat turned Rita upside down and the ruby slid out of her pants.

Spike and Whitey took Roddy and Rita to see
The Toad.

"At last, I can return the ruby to my collection
of royal treasures," The Toad said.

"I'm the one who found your ruby," Roddy
said and asked The Toad to help him get home.

"That depends. What do you think of my
collection?" asked The Toad.

"It's amusing," Roddy replied.

"What!" shouted The Toad. He didn't think his collection was funny.

Frightened, Roddy stumbled. He bumped into something and knocked everything over.

"Ice him! Ice them both!" The Toad bellowed.

Roddy and Rita were chained in a blender in the dreaded Ice Room.

"They're going to freeze us!" Roddy exclaimed.

Rita had a paper clip in her back pocket. She used it to free them.

She and Roddy climbed out of the blender. At the last moment, they pushed Spike and Whitey in. When The Toad saw that he'd frozen his own men, he was furious!

"After them!" he cried.

Rita and Roddy ran through The Toad's lair, looking for a way to escape. Suddenly, Rita spotted a power cable. That gave her an idea. She yanked the cable from its socket and the lights went out.

She hurried over to a window, leaned out, and looped the cable over a power line.

Roddy saw that she was about to get away without him.

"Wait for me!" he said.

Roddy jumped. He clung to Rita's belt as they swung out over the water.

Once they were safe, Roddy and Rita sailed the *Jammy Dodger* to Rita's house. Rita told her father and her brother Liam that Roddy had promised to give her a jewel if she helped him get home.

Liam said that The Toad was offering a reward for the two of them.

"You should tell The Toad it's all Roddy's fault," he said. "Then you could get the money."

Roddy overheard the conversation and it hurt his feelings. How could Rita turn him in after all they had been through?

Roddy decided to steal the *Jammy Dodger* and find his own way home. When Rita saw him sailing away she chased after him—riding a rubber duck!

"You double-crosser!" Rita yelled. "How could you steal my boat?"

"I'm the double-crosser?" Roddy shouted. "You were going to sell me to The Toad!"

"I was not. That was my brother's idea. I was going to help you get home," Rita answered. "But you're not fit to ride in my boat!"

Rita made Roddy ride on the duck. But she did give him a ukulele for a paddle.

Roddy begged Rita to forgive him. He even sang her a song. Finally, she agreed to help him again.

The Toad was still searching for Roddy and Rita.
He called his cousin Le Frog for help.

"*Bonjour*, cousin," said Le Frog. "How can I help
you?"

"I need you to find the two rats who've stolen my
cable. Once it is returned my plan will be complete.
I can wash away these cursed rats once and for all!"
whispered The Toad.

Just then, he pulled out a scrapbook full of old
photos.

"Not the scrapbook again!" muttered Le Frog.

"Once I was the prince's favorite pet. Then he was given a rat for his birthday and I was flushed down the toilet into this filthy sewer!" The Toad bellowed.

"Calm down, cousin. I will get your cable back," said Le Frog.

Later that day, Roddy and Rita were surrounded by Le Frog and his hench-frogs. The frogs were ready to attack, but the boat began to tilt. The *Jammy Dodger* was caught in swirling rapids!

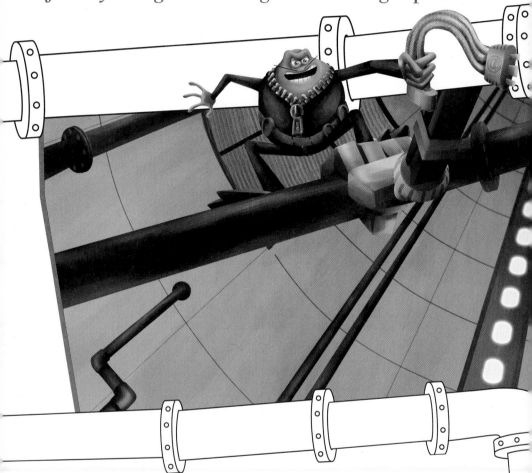

The boat began to plunge down a waterfall. Rita grabbed hold of the ship with one hand and held on to Roddy's collar with the other. Just then Le Frog snatched the cable from around Rita's waist. As the *Dodger* fell, Roddy grabbed a floating plastic bag. The bag filled with air and lifted them up just like a balloon.

A gust of air carried them up through a sewer pipe to the surface. Suddenly, Rita and Roddy were flying over Kensington toward Roddy's house.

Back home, Roddy gave Rita a pair of ruby earrings. She thanked him and went back to the sewers.

Roddy was sad to see her leave. He realized
that he might have a cage like a palace and the
finest clothes, but he didn't have any friends.

So Roddy did something he never thought
he'd do—he flushed himself down the toilet! He
landed back in the sewer just in time. The Toad
had caught Rita! Roddy tried to rescue her, but
he was caught, too!

"Did you think you could make a fool of me?" asked The Toad. "I have my cable and now my plan is complete. While everyone watches the World Cup, I've opened the floodgates to the city. When the people up top flush their toilets at half-time, this city of rats will be washed away!"

"We've got to stop him!" cried Rita. Just then, they heard a loud flushing sound—it was half-time!

"You're too late! You rats are finished!" The Toad cackled.

Hundreds of slugs poured out of the sewer as a giant wave approached the city!

Roddy and Rita took off running but The Toad was close on their heels. Suddenly, Roddy stopped. He noticed the pipes under his feet. He tugged at one and ripped it loose. Freezing gas shot out of the end. The Toad and the giant wave were frozen solid!

"Roddy, you're a hero!" Rita exclaimed.

"Thanks, Rita," Roddy said. "But I was wondering . . . I mean, I'm all alone where I live. Do you think that you might, well, need a first mate for the new *Jammy Dodger*?"

"You're hired," Rita said. She gave Roddy a big hug.